Buddies

Dazzle Makes a Wish

Cynthia Lord

illustrated by

Stephanie Graegin

CANDLEWICK PRESS

Text copyright © 2023 by Cynthia Lord
Illustrations copyright © 2023 by Stephanie Graegin

First edition 2023

Library of Congress Catalog Card Number 2022908640
ISBN 978-1-5362-1356-0 (hardcover)
ISBN 978-1-5362-3241-7 (paperback)

22 23 24 25 26 27 LBM 10 9 8 7 6 5 4 3 2 1

Printed in Melrose Park, IL, USA

This book was typeset in Sabon.
The illustrations were created digitally.

Candlewick Press
99 Dover Street
Somerville, Massachusetts 02144

www.candlewick.com

MIX
Paper | Supporting
responsible forestry
FSC® C103098

For Gregory
CL

For my nieces
SG

CHAPTER ONE
Dazzle

For weeks the unicorn waited on the toy store shelf. Families came and went, but no one bought the snow-white unicorn with a twisty horn and a sparkly pink tail. On his tag, it said his name was Dazzle. It also said that unicorns can grant wishes, but only for someone with a good heart.

Dazzle didn't know if he could grant a wish for himself. But he thought it was worth a try. So every night, he made the same wish.

I wish for a home and a child of my own.

One day a grandmother came into the toy store. She looked at the shelves of stuffed animals. Then she pointed to Dazzle. "Is this toy good for babies?" she asked the store clerk. "I just learned that I will be a grandmother in the spring."

"Oh, how wonderful!" the store clerk said. "Yes, a baby will love this."

The grandmother bought Dazzle and took him home.

My wish is coming true! Dazzle thought. At the grandmother's house, he spent long weeks sitting in a rocking chair, waiting for the baby to be born.

Until one day, the grandmother picked him up. *Today is the day!* Dazzle thought as she carried him outside.

But there was no baby outside.

On the front lawn, tables were piled high with old things. A sign on a tree said YARD SALE TODAY.

Dazzle was dropped onto a table with a lamp, some plant pots, a stack of books, and a rusty hammer. The grandmother crossed out his toy store price and wrote *$3.00* on his tag.

Dazzle felt his horn droop. A few of his tail sparkles fell onto the table. He'd heard whispers about yard sales from other toys at the toy store. Yard sales were a second chance for old and unloved toys.

But I'm not old, Dazzle thought. *And how can I need a second chance? I've never even had a first chance!*

A woman came to the table. She turned some pages in one of the old books. Then she saw Dazzle. She smiled as she read his tag.

"Are you sure you want to sell this unicorn?" the woman asked. "He looks brand-new."

The grandmother nodded. "He is brand-new. But we found out that our first grandchild will be a boy. And I'm not sure that a boy would like a unicorn."

"All children like unicorns."

"Well, this toy sheds!" the grandmother added. "It might not even be safe for a baby!" She brushed Dazzle's sparkles off the table.

"I'm Anne, the children's librarian at the library," the woman told the grandmother. "We have some toys at the library called Book Buddies. Children read to them and borrow them. This unicorn will be a perfect Book Buddy."

"Since it's for the library, I'll make you a deal," the grandmother said. "You can have it for two dollars."

Dazzle looked at a piece of glitter on the ground. He had thought people would like finding some surprise sparkles.

On the way to her car, Anne whispered in his ear. "Everyone at the library will love you."

A library will be better than a yard sale, Dazzle thought. But still, he couldn't help feeling sad.

He wasn't getting a home and a child of his own.

His wish hadn't come true after all.

CHAPTER TWO

At the Library

Dazzle was right. The library was much better than a yard sale. He was played with by lots of children, both boys and girls. They read him stories and brushed his sparkly pink tail. Dazzle loved being borrowed and taken on adventures—even if he had to be washed often to keep his colors bright.

Something was missing, though.

Borrowing isn't the same as belonging, Dazzle thought. *And a library is not the same as a home.*

Every week, the Book Buddies looked forward to story time. On those mornings, the library was filled with children and their families. It was a good chance to be borrowed.

Today a new family had come. There was a mother, a girl, and a little boy.

"Hello!" Anne greeted them. "Welcome to the library!"

"Thank you," the mother said. "We've just moved here. We're out exploring our new neighborhood today. These are my children, Maya and Mateo."

"I'm Anne. I'm so glad you're here," she said. "Story time will begin in a few minutes if you want to come."

Maya pointed to Dazzle. "Mama, look! There's a unicorn!"

"His name is Dazzle," Anne said. "These toys are Book Buddies. They love to be played with and read to. And they can be borrowed and taken home. You just need a library card. I can sign you up for library cards after story time."

"Thank you," Mama said. "We'd like that. Wouldn't we, kids?"

Maya nodded. She looked carefully at every Book Buddy on the shelf. There was a gray

flying squirrel, an owl, a brown bear, a tiny felt mouse, a garden gnome with a white beard and a pointy purple hat, a black-and-white chicken and her yellow chick, and two dolls. One doll was a princess and another had black braids.

But the unicorn was Maya's favorite. "I'd like to borrow Dazzle, please."

"And I want to borrow the wizard!" Mateo said, pointing.

"That's Nugget," Anne said. "His tag said he's a garden gnome, but you can pretend he's a wizard. He'd love that!"

"He's Wizard Wonderful!" Mateo said.

"After story time we will sign up for library cards," Mama said. "You can each borrow a Book Buddy and some books to read to them."

"Today's story time is about squirrels. So Piper is our guest of honor." Anne took the flying squirrel off the Book Buddies shelf. "The first book I'm reading is *Scaredy Squirrel*!"

"I know that book!" Maya grinned. Moving to a new place meant everything was different and new. So it was nice to see the cover of *Scaredy Squirrel*. It felt like seeing an old friend.

"Do you want to go to story time?" Mama asked her.

Maya did want to go. She liked to read to herself, but it was work, too. Listening to someone else read was only fun. It was easier to imagine the story and enjoy the art.

The other children leaving with Anne looked young, though. They were closer to Mateo's age than her age.

"If Mateo wants to." Maya shrugged like it didn't matter. But inside, she hoped Mateo would say yes.

"Okay," Mateo said. "Let's go."

CHAPTER THREE

The Toys

After the children left, Dazzle shook his tail. He hoped any loose glitter would fall off. He didn't want to shed on Maya.

"You're so lucky, Dazzle!" Lilyanna the princess doll said. "I was hoping Maya would pick me!"

"Such a nice new family," Olive the hen clucked. "Dazzle and Nugget, you can help them feel at home."

Dazzle was proud to have such an important job.

"I don't answer to that name," Nugget said. "I'm Wizard Wonderful now." He waved his arm. "Abracadabra!"

"Abra-what?" Roger the chick asked.

"It's wizard talk," Nugget said. "I'm casting a spell."

Homer the owl shook his head. "Magicians say 'Abracadabra.' Not wizards. And you're not a wizard or a magician. You're a garden gnome."

"Not anymore," Nugget said. "I'm Wizard Wonderful! Mateo said so."

"Yes, but that's just pretend," Homer said. "Children can pretend anything they want, but it doesn't change the facts. It doesn't change who we are inside."

"A child could pretend *you* were a penguin," Nugget said.

"How foolish!" Homer said. "I am brown. Penguins are black and white."

Nugget waved his arm. "Poof! You're a penguin."

"Now you're just being silly," Homer said.

"It's not silly, it's pretending," Nugget said. "Anything is possible when you pretend. Haven't you ever wanted to be a penguin, Homer?"

"Never," Homer said.

"But it's fun!" Nugget said. "It's boring being yourself all the time."

"Not when you're a princess," Lilyanna said. "Princesses are never boring."

"Dazzle, I'll cast a spell for you next!" Nugget said. "What would you like to be?"

Dazzle thought. He remembered how he had wished every night at the toy store.

I wish for a home and a child of my own.

And that wish hadn't come true. As a Book Buddy, lots of children loved him, but he didn't belong to any of them for keeps. *Maybe if I didn't shed, the grandmother would've kept me.*

"Not so sparkly," Dazzle said quietly.

"Shh!" Homer said. "I hear the children coming. Story time must be over."

Maya was the first child through the door. She ran right to the Book Buddies shelf and picked up Dazzle. She handed Nugget to Mateo. "Now

18

let's get some books. Mama said we could each pick four."

Dazzle was excited by the picture books that Maya chose. She even chose one of Dazzle's favorite books about magical creatures. It had a beautiful white unicorn on the cover.

Maya put Dazzle and her books on Anne's desk. "I'd like to check these out, please."

Anne gave Mama some forms to fill out. Then she got three brand-new library cards from her desk. One for Mama. One for Maya. One for Mateo.

Maya touched the shiny card. It was exciting to have her own library card.

"I have something else for you." Anne pulled two small books off the shelf behind her desk. "Each Book Buddy has a journal. You can read about Dazzle's and Nugget's adventures at other children's houses. And you can write and draw their adventures at your house."

Maya opened Dazzle's journal. His tag had been taped on the first page. Maya smiled as she read the words.

"It says that unicorns can grant wishes, but only for someone with a good heart," she said.

Anne nodded. "What would you wish for?"

Maya touched Dazzle's twisty horn. Moving to a new home was exciting, but it had been hard, too. She had left all her friends behind.

"I wish for a friend," she said.

CHAPTER FOUR

Maya's Room

At home, Maya put her library books on top of her dresser. She put her new library card carefully in her top dresser drawer so she'd know right where to find it.

Maya's new room didn't feel like home yet. Moving boxes were still stacked up along one wall. She and Mama hadn't had time to unpack everything, only the most important things. Maya's bed was ready to sleep in. Her clothes were in the dresser. And her favorite toy was set up in the corner.

It was a special doll's treehouse that her grandfather had made. From the front, it looked like a tree stump, but there were tiny steps leading up to a red front door that opened and closed. There was even a bucket on a string that could be filled with little things and pulled up to a small porch.

The back of the stump had been hollowed out to make rooms. There was a kitchen and bedrooms with furniture, just the right size for Maya's fairies.

"The fairies will be excited to meet more magical creatures!" she told Mateo.

Mateo brought Nugget to the treehouse. "Wake up, fairies! I am Wizard Wonderful. I've come to say hi!"

Maya set Dazzle up in front of the treehouse, too. His nose was right near the door. Then Maya went around to the back of the treehouse and made the front door open. Three fairy faces appeared in the doorway.

They were the most beautiful toys that Dazzle had ever seen.

One fairy had dark skin and long brown hair. Her dress was made of blue lace, the color of a summer sky. The lace was trimmed with gold. "This is Opal," Maya said.

The second fairy had pale skin and yellow hair. Her dress was raspberry-colored, trimmed with silver. "This is Ruby."

The third fairy had a tan face and short brown hair. He wore a pine cone hat, a mossy green shirt, brown leggings, and boots. "And this is Pinecone," Mateo said.

"Fairies, meet Dazzle and Wizard Wonderful," Maya said. "They're magical, too. Unicorns can grant wishes and wizards cast spells."

"Fairies can fly," Mateo said. "And they have treasures!"

"Do you want to pretend the fairies are having a party to welcome Wizard Wonderful and Dazzle to the neighborhood?" Maya asked.

"Yes!" Mateo grinned. "Can I play with Pinecone?"

"Okay, but you have to be gentle with him," Maya said. "Remember that the fairies aren't made strong like regular toys."

"I promise," Mateo said. "I'll be very, very gentle."

Maya gave Pinecone to Mateo. "And Ruby and Opal are going to make invitations to the party." She looked at the moving boxes and sighed. "If I can remember which box has my art pencils in it."

Mama looked into the room. "Kids, will you help me? My new boss just called. She is coming over today. There is some paperwork that we need to do. It shouldn't take very long, but it must be done today."

Maya nodded. "Don't worry, Mama. I'll take care of Mateo."

"And I'll take care of Maya," Mateo said.

"Thank you!" Mama said. "But there is one more thing. My boss must bring her daughter with her. Her name is Isabelle. Will you two play with Isabelle while we work?"

"Yes!" Maya was so excited that she jumped to her feet. "Mateo, let's wait for Isabelle at the front door so she'll feel welcome right away!"

"I knew I could count on you," Mama said.

Maya couldn't believe it! A new friend was coming over.

Her wish was already coming true.

CHAPTER FIVE

The Fairies

Dazzle couldn't stop looking at the three little fairies. They were perfect and beautiful, with wings so thin he could almost see through them.

"I'm sorry to stare," Dazzle said. "But I've never met a fairy before."

"We're from Mexico," said Pinecone proudly. "Maya's grandparents live there. Her grandmother bought us for her birthday."

"Her grandfather made our treehouse," Ruby said. "We have furniture and toy food."

"And treasure!" Opal said. "*Real* treasure."

"Wow," Dazzle said. "It's so nice to meet you. Nugget—I mean, Wizard Wonderful—and I are Book Buddies. Maya and Mateo borrowed us from the library."

"Borrowed?" Opal asked. "What does that mean?"

"We can go home with a child for two weeks," Nugget said. "Then we are returned to the library so another child can borrow us."

"You don't have a home of your own?" Ruby asked.

Dazzle didn't know how to answer that. "I was bought for a baby, but it didn't work out," he finally said.

He didn't want to talk about the yard sale.

"You're lucky that it didn't work out," Opal said. "Babies are terrible creatures! They grab you. They hug you. They drool. They put toys in their mouths!"

"We have tiny jewels on our clothes and shoes that could be swallowed!" Ruby said.

"We aren't made for babies, either," said Pinecone. "It says so on our box. Ages eight and up."

"That's why Mateo can only play with us when Maya is there," Opal said. "She makes sure he follows the fairy rules."

"What are the fairy rules?" Dazzle asked.

"Never play with us roughly," Pinecone said.

"And never outside," Opal said.

"Goodness, no!" Ruby looked shocked. "It would be a disaster if we got dirty! We cannot be washed! Maya brings the outside inside to us. It's much safer that way."

Opal nodded. "We have an acorn, tiny shells, a sand dollar, feathers, and pretty rocks."

"They're our treasures," Pinecone said. "Our most special things."

Dazzle found it strange that the fairies' treasures were from outdoors but they'd only ever been indoors. "I'm glad I can be hugged and washed," he said. "And it's fun to go outside."

"Well, maybe it's okay for toys like *you*," Ruby said. "Toys with, um—"

"Stuffing," Pinecone finished.

"Not to brag, but we're *collectible*," said Opal.

"What does that mean?" Dazzle asked.

"Children can collect us," Pinecone said. "We fairies come in different colors and kinds. And it's fun to have more."

"And more!" Ruby said.

"And more!" Opal said.

"We're made to be shown off and looked at," Pinecone said. "Some serious collectors keep their fairies in glass cases. Those fairies stay perfect and never get dusty."

"Some people have hundreds of us!" Opal said.

"Hundreds!" Ruby said.

Dazzle couldn't even imagine that. Living in a glass case didn't sound like fun to him. "Don't you ever have adventures?"

"Oh no! Adventures are dangerous!" Opal said. "We might be damaged."

"What do you do for fun then?" Nugget asked.

"We pose," Opal said. "We have magnets on the bottoms of our feet so we can stand on our magic metal leaves." She lifted one foot off her metal leaf. "See? I can stand like this for hours."

"Days!" Pinecone said.

"Months!" Ruby said. "And we have wire in our arms and legs." She raised her arm. "See? I'm waving!"

Dazzle thought the fairies were very proud of themselves.

"I hear footsteps!" Pinecone said. "The children are coming! Everyone look beautiful!"

"Maya's new friend will be excited to see us—her friends always are," Opal said. She smoothed her dress so it would glimmer.

Nugget straightened his hat.

Dazzle shook his tail so it would be fluffy. A few sparkles fell off his tail. He hoped Maya wouldn't mind.

The door opened. "And this is my room!" Maya said. "It's a bit messy because I'm still unpacking."

A new girl stepped into the room. She looked about Maya's age.

But she didn't look happy.

CHAPTER SIX
Isabelle

Isabelle looked at the picture books on Maya's dresser.

"We went to the library this morning," Maya explained. "These are the books that I checked out. We can read them if you want."

"I only read chapter books now," Isabelle said. "But that was nice of you to get some books for your little brother."

Maya opened her mouth. She didn't want to tell Isabelle that she had borrowed the books for herself, though. What if Isabelle made fun of her?

Maya closed her mouth.

"And we borrowed Wizard Wonderful and Dazzle, too." Mateo ran over to get Nugget. "They're Book Buddies. The fairies are going to have a party to welcome them to the neighborhood!"

"We waited for you to play, too," Maya said.

Isabelle sighed. "I don't really play with stuffed animals anymore."

Oh. Maya looked around her room for something else to play. She wished she had unpacked more toys.

Isabelle gasped.

Maya turned to see Isabelle staring at the treehouse. "What's this?" Isabelle asked, her eyes wide.

"It's a treehouse that my grandfather made," Maya said proudly. "And my grandmother sent me the little fairies. Their names are Ruby, Opal, and Pinecone."

"I'll play with the fairies," Isabelle said. "You two can play with the stuffed animals. But let's pretend something more exciting than just a party."

"I want to play a party," Mateo said.

Maya looked from Mateo to Isabelle. She couldn't make them both happy. Isabelle was only there for a few hours, though. And they had finally found something Isabelle wanted to do.

"Mama said we needed to share," Maya told Mateo. "We can play a party later. Okay?"

Mateo pouted.

Maya turned to Isabelle. "What do *you* want to play?"

Isabelle looked at the Book Buddies. "Stories are always more exciting when something goes wrong," she said.

Wrong? Maya didn't like when things went wrong. It might be exciting, but it was a *bad* kind of exciting.

Maya took a deep breath. It was just pretending, though. Things didn't have to go wrong for real.

"Okay," she said. "What should go wrong?"

Isabelle smiled. "Everything."

CHAPTER SEVEN

Everything Goes Wrong

Let's pretend Dazzle is the fairies' unicorn," Isabelle said. "But then one day an evil wizard came to town."

"Wizard Wonderful is a *good* wizard," Mateo said.

"It's more exciting if he's evil," Isabelle said. "He can be called Wicked Wizard."

Mateo pouted at Maya.

Maya didn't like that idea, either. But if she told Isabelle she didn't want to play Isabelle's way, what would happen?

Would Isabelle tell her mother? Would Mama get in trouble?

Would Isabelle not want to be her friend?

"It's just pretend," Maya said. "Okay, Mateo?"

"No," Mateo said.

But Isabelle wasn't listening. "Pinecone was trying to get away." Isabelle took Pinecone off

his metal leaf and tugged his legs open to ride on Dazzle's back.

Maya cringed.

"But Wicked Wizard cast a spell on Dazzle to make him start bucking!" Isabelle made Dazzle buck hard. Pinecone flew off Dazzle's back and into the air.

Maya jumped up to catch him. "Be careful!"

But it was too late. Pinecone bounced onto the unpacked boxes and fell behind them.

Isabelle laughed. "That was a big spell!"

Maya didn't think it was funny. She looked at the boxes. Where was he? She might have to move all the boxes to find him.

"Ruby and Opal tried to save him," Isabelle said. "But the evil wizard captured them and locked them up in fairy jail. And he stole their leaves so they can't stand up!"

Isabelle yanked Ruby off her metal leaf. Ruby's tiny foot got stuck and one of her jewels ripped off her shoe.

"Dazzle can save them," Mateo said.

Isabelle grabbed Dazzle. "Dazzle charged at Wicked Wizard as he was locking the door to the jail. But the wizard turned around just in time to cast another spell. 'Freeze!' he yelled. Now Dazzle was frozen and couldn't move!"

"That's it! I'm not playing anymore," Mateo said. "I'm going to find Mama."

"Wait, Mateo!" Maya said. "Mama is working. We said we'd take care of each other, remember?"

But Mateo was already out the door.

"Come on, Isabelle," Maya said. "We have to stop him. I'm supposed to be watching him."

"All right," Isabelle said. "But I'm leaving the evil wizard right here to guard the jail."

CHAPTER EIGHT

Damaged

As soon as the children were gone, Ruby sobbed, "I've lost my shoe sparkle. I'm damaged!"

"Don't worry. Maya won't mind that you lost one sparkle," Dazzle said. "I lose glitter all the time and children still love me."

"You don't understand," Ruby wailed. "Collectibles have to be perfect."

Opal nodded. "If we're damaged, we're not worth as much. We're marked down in price. Or maybe even thrown away."

Dazzle knew what it was like to be marked down. He knew how it felt to be given away. "I do understand a bit," he said softly. "All I ever wished for was a home and a child of my own. I wished it over and over. Then a grandmother bought me. I thought my wish had come true. But she said that I shed." He took a deep breath. "I was sold at a yard sale."

Ruby and Opal gasped.

"I didn't think I would ever be loved," Dazzle said.

"Loved?" Opal said. "What does that mean?"

For the first time, Dazzle felt sorry for the fairies. "It's hard to explain," he said. "But it's a warm, happy feeling. You know you belong with someone and they belong with you."

"Are you loved?" Opal asked.

Dazzle didn't even need to think about it. "I'm loved by Anne and the children at the library."

"And your Book Buddy friends!" Nugget said. "We love you, too. You belong with us."

Dazzle smiled.

"You wished for one child—but you got a whole library full!" Nugget said. "So maybe your wish did come true, but in a surprise way."

Dazzle thought about it. Could Nugget be right? Could wishes be sneaky like that?

"Pinecone, Opal, and I belong together," Ruby said. "But now he's lost!"

"I'm sorry I made Pinecone disappear," Nugget said. "I wish I wasn't a wizard anymore. Magic is trouble."

Dazzle smiled. "You don't even need a unicorn to make that wish come true. Remember what Homer said? Children can pretend anything, but it doesn't change who you are inside. Inside, you're still Nugget the garden gnome."

Nugget smiled back. "If I'm not really a wizard, then there's no spell. Right?"

Dazzle nodded. "Yes. It's just pretend."

"And if there's no spell—?" Nugget started.

"I'm not really frozen!" Dazzle shook himself and pranced around the room. As he swung his tail, a few sparkles flew into the air.

"We're not really in jail!" Opal said.

"But Pinecone is still lost," Ruby said.

Dazzle looked toward the boxes. He could see Pinecone's foot barely sticking out from behind one of the big boxes. It was so tiny. He didn't think Maya would notice it. Poor Pinecone might be trapped there until the boxes were all unpacked.

"I wish I could help," Dazzle said.

But how? As he was thinking, he saw something shiny on the floor. It was one of his sparkles.

It gave him an idea.

CHAPTER NINE

The Snapping Point

Maya had to make many promises to Mateo. It was the only way he'd agree to come back to her room and not interrupt Mama.

Maya promised she'd read her library books to him.

She promised he could have extra crackers at snack time.

"And I can play with Wizard Wonderful my own way," Mateo said.

"Yes," Maya promised.

She felt stretched almost to the snapping point. She'd been so excited to have Isabelle over, but she was tired of everything going wrong. Maya wanted to make everything right again. She wanted to fix Ruby's shoe and find Pinecone and hug Dazzle and play with Mateo.

She wanted Isabelle to go home.

Isabelle had more ideas. "I know that Dazzle is a boy," she said. "But I have the best name for a girl unicorn! Let's pretend Dazzle is a girl and her name is Sparkle Dewberry. It has more glitz."

Maya looked at Dazzle. He didn't need a new name. He didn't need more glitz. Maya's patience had been stretched as far as it could go.

And then it *snapped*.

"No," Maya said.

Isabelle and Mateo both looked up.

"No," Maya said louder. "I don't want to play that way. His name is Dazzle and he's a boy unicorn."

"But your mom said you had to share," Isabelle said.

Maya nodded. "Sharing means playing together, not one person deciding everything. I'm deciding that Dazzle is perfect, just the way he is. Mateo has decided that Wizard Wonderful is a good wizard. You can decide about the fairies. But only if you play gently with them. Or we'll have to play something else."

Isabelle looked shocked.

"Mateo and I want to pretend that the toys are having a party," Maya said. "But you can choose an exciting part. A *good* exciting part."

Isabelle didn't answer right away. Then she said, "Maybe Pinecone went to find food for the party and got lost? So now they have to rescue him."

Maya nodded. "That's a very good exciting part!"

"I'm sorry I threw him," Isabelle said. "I'll help you find him."

Maya looked at the boxes. There were so many of them. *Where to begin?*

A spot of pink glimmered. It almost looked like one of Dazzle's sparkles, but how could it have gotten all the way over there?

Maya went over to take a closer look, and that's when she saw something sticking out from behind one of the boxes. It was a tiny foot.

"Pinecone!" Maya cried. "Don't worry, we'll rescue you!"

CHAPTER TEN

A Very Good Exciting

Isabelle put Ruby and Opal carefully on Dazzle's back. Maya held Nugget on his back, too. Then she made Dazzle gallop, carrying the toys to the edge of the moving box.

"Don't worry, Pinecone! The other toys are coming to rescue you!" Mateo said.

Together the children helped the toys pull Pinecone out from behind the box. Maya held him in her hand. It was so good to have him back.

She handed him to Isabelle.

"I'll be very gentle with him," Isabelle promised.

"Hooray! Now they can have a party!" Mateo said.

"It'll be a Welcome *and* a Welcome Back party!" Maya smiled. "A party for new and old friends."

"At the party I think fairies would serve acorn tea and berries! And they'd—" Isabelle stopped. She looked at Maya and Mateo. "But what do you think?"

Maya smiled. "I like that. How about little cakes for dessert?"

"Chocolate cakes!" Mateo said.

Isabelle nodded. "That sounds perfect! Acorn tea, berries, and chocolate cakes."

Dazzle and Nugget didn't fit in the little treehouse kitchen, so the party was held in the middle of Maya's room.

Maya put a blanket on the floor. Isabelle put the toy food on the blanket. Mateo brought out the fairies' treasure box.

Maya put Ruby's shoe sparkle and some of Dazzle's glitter in the treasure box. "The fairies can keep these to remember how Dazzle, Wizard Wonderful, Ruby, and Opal saved

Pinecone from Box Mountain. And they all became friends and had a party."

"And then they wanted to hear a story," Mateo said. "Maya, I'll get the book about magical creatures. You can read to them!"

Mateo put the book in front of Maya.

Maya took a deep breath. Even if Isabelle made fun of her, she wanted to tell the truth. "I didn't borrow these books for Mateo," she said. "I love art and beautiful books. I picked these books for myself."

Isabelle looked surprised, but then she nodded at Maya. "It's a really pretty book. Ruby will turn the pages for you." Isabelle made Ruby fly over to open the book cover.

Mateo set the toys up in front of the book so everyone could see. Then Maya started to read. They were all having so much fun that they didn't hear Mama and Isabelle's mom come into the room.

"We've finished our work," Mama said.

Maya had wanted Isabelle to go home, but now she was sad to see her go. "Can Isabelle come back and play again soon?"

Mama nodded. "Of course."

Isabelle grinned. "Next time I'll bring a few of my toys to meet yours. They can have another party."

"That would be exciting!" Maya said. "A *very* good exciting!"

CHAPTER ELEVEN

Wishes Are Sneaky

Two weeks later, most of Maya's moving boxes had been unpacked. Maya's new house was starting to feel like home. Isabelle had been over to play two more times.

And it was time for Dazzle and Nugget to return to the library.

Maya couldn't wait to show Dazzle's journal to Anne. "Dazzle made lots of new friends!" she said. "And he was one of *my* first friends here."

Anne smiled. "Wow! Look at all the fun he had at your house!"

Maya had filled four pages! She'd drawn Dazzle, Nugget, Opal, Ruby, and Pinecone sitting on a tablecloth having a picnic.

Dazzle, Nugget, Opal Ruby, and Pinecone had a picnic.

Dazzle loves stories.

Dazzle hearing a story.

Dazzle playing with the fairies.

Dazzle and Nugget exploring the outdoors.

Dazzle having a bath in the washing machine.

"Such wonderful adventures!" Anne said. "Thank you for taking such good care of him."

Maya gave Dazzle a big hug as she carried him to the Book Buddies' shelf. "Thank you for making my wish come true," she whispered. "I love you, Dazzle."

Dazzle felt that warm feeling inside. He loved Maya, too. In fact, he loved all the children he met at the library. And they loved him back, just the way he was: a white unicorn with a sparkly pink tail that shed glitter sometimes.

Nugget was right, he thought. His wish had come true in a surprise way. His hard start had turned into a happy ending.

He smiled at his Book Buddy friends.

It felt so good to be home.

CYNTHIA LORD is the author of award-winning middle-grade fiction titles such as the Newbery Honor Book *Rules, Touch Blue, Half a Chance, A Handful of Stars,* and *Because of the Rabbit.* She is also the author of the Hot Rod Hamster picture book and early reader series as well as the Shelter Pet Squad chapter book series. Cynthia Lord lives in Maine.

STEPHANIE GRAEGIN is the author-illustrator of *Little Fox in the Forest* and the illustrator of many other picture books, including *You Were the First* by Patricia MacLachlan and *Water in the Park* by Emily Jenkins. Stephanie Graegin lives in Brooklyn.

Look for the next installment in the
Book Buddies series coming Spring 2024!

Book  Buddies

Roger Takes a Chance

Meet the Book Buddies, toys that can
be checked out from the library,
just like books. For the Book Buddies,
every borrowing is a new adventure!